The Amber Giant

Handersen Publishing, LLC
Lincoln, Nebraska

The Amber Giant

Text copyright © 2017 Giulietta M. Spudich
Cover copyright © 2017 Handersen Publishing, LLC
Cover Design by Nichole Hansen
Interior Design by Nichole Hansen

Manufactured in the United States of America.

Summary: Eleven-year-old Caroline travels to Kathmandu, Nepal, where high in the Himalayas she discovers the Amber Giant, a mythical creature who has been asleep for a thousand years. She awakens him, and suddenly has her very own giant.

Library of Congress Control Number: 2017900395
Handersen Publishing, LLC, Lincoln, Nebraska

ISBN-13: 9781941429495

Publisher Website: www.handersenpublishing.com
Publisher Email: editors@handersenpublishing.com

Dedicated to Sammy on his eleventh birthday.
This is the story of the Amber Giant.

The Amber Giant

Giulietta M. Spudich

Handersen Publishing LLC
Lincoln, Nebraska

Chapter One

It was a quiet Sunday evening in Tarrytown, New York. Caroline, eleven, and Sammy, eight, were playing a board game. Their mom, Miranda, was busy singing and cooking in the kitchen. Their dad, David, was out.

Caroline was getting bored. It was the third game already. Sammy giggled as he jumped over her piece with his and made his way down the path leading to the goal.

"So what if you won?" Caroline sighed.

"You mean, again," her brother replied with a grin from ear-to-ear. "I won *again*."

As Sammy danced his victory dance, Caroline thought about what to do next. Her mom was still singing, which meant she wasn't paying attention to what she and her brother were doing.

Caroline had wanted to investigate Dad's study for weeks. He was an archaeologist, and he was working on a cool new project. Caroline had overheard him on the phone, and he kept mentioning giants. The only problem was, they weren't allowed in Dad's study.

Caroline nudged her little brother and pointed to the back of the house.

Sammy's eyes lit up.

"Dad's room?" he said too loud.

Caroline shushed him with a finger to her lips. They crept down the hall and opened the door.

When Caroline turned on the light, she gasped in excitement at the dusty room full of books. Maps were scattered on the desk and floor. She loved old books and maps. She wished she could read all the books, even spend a few nights in the study.

Caroline ran her finger along the spines of the books, all packed together on the bookshelf. She especially loved big, dusty books.

Sammy got too close to a book and sneezed.

Caroline shushed him, then read the title of the old book he was looking at.

The Amber Giant.

Sammy looked up at her.

3

They didn't need to speak. Both of them knew the book required further investigation.

Together, they pulled it out of the old, wooden bookshelf. A few neighboring books and papers fell down with a crash, and Caroline winced at the noise.

Would Mom hear?

Caroline froze.

When Caroline heard her mom's singing, she knew their efforts had gone undetected. She gave Sammy a thumbs up. They both heaved the book onto the desk. Clouds of dust lifted from the pages when they opened it.

Caroline ran her fingers over a page with unusual letters in a strange font. Her fingers traced the illustration of the mountain peak covered with snow. She sounded out a few words that were hard to read in the strange lettering.

4

"In the valley between peak H-123 and peak H-124..." she read, as her finger ran under the words.

"Be careful, Caroline! You'll tear it," Sammy whispered. He grabbed her wrist and tried to pull her hand away.

"I won't. I'm being careful. Get back, I can't see anything but your hair." Caroline rolled her dark eyes. Sammy's hair was always in the way.

"I'm not blocking it," he argued, his voice growing louder. His brown curls blocked out Caroline's view of the page as he bent closer to the book.

"You *are*. I can't even see the mountain anymore."

"Mountain?" Sammy leaned closer to the page. Caroline couldn't see it at all now.

"Back up!" Her words came out much louder than she intended.

5

"Kids!" Their mom's high voice called from the kitchen. "You better not be in your dad's study."

They exchanged looks with wide, alarmed eyes.

"We're not in the study, Mom!" Sammy yelled back.

"*Shh!*" Caroline said. "You'll give us away. She'll know we're in here." Caroline slammed the book shut, releasing another cloud of dust. With all her might, she picked it up and started to carry it out of the room.

"What are you doing?" Sammy stood in front of her. "You can't take the book. Dad will know."

"He'll never notice," Caroline argued. "Look how messy this place is!"

There were papers and books stacked high on the wooden desk. More were scattered all over the floor.

"We'll get in trouble." Sammy grabbed hold of the book, and pulled.

"Kids!" Mom called again, and this time she sounded louder and closer.

"Sammy, let go!" Caroline commanded, playing tug-of-war with the book.

They both jumped at the sound of an angry voice.

"What are you two doing in here?" Mom said, looking furious.

Both Caroline and Sammy looked down at their feet, ashamed about sneaking around Dad's study.

"Put that book back where you found it. And go up to your rooms, both of you."

Caroline pushed her brother, and he stuck his tongue out at her.

"I can't believe you're double digits, Caroline," Mom scolded. "Act your age." Her

mother's dark eyes matched the color of her curly hair. Caroline and Sammy both got their mother's messy curls and dark eyes.

"Oh, all right," Caroline said as she stormed out of the study.

"Caroline?" Her mom's voice sounded strained.

Caroline turned with a smile she hoped was innocent.

"Put that book on the table," Mom said. "Then you can go to your room and make your bed."

"Fine." Caroline dropped the book onto the table with a thump. She took one long look at the cover. Framed in an elaborate, golden circle was a hairy, serious-faced creature with small eyes, a heavy forehead, and a large, pitted nose. The beast had beautiful, yellow-gold fur.

"The Amber Giant," Caroline said, enjoying the sound of it.

"Caroline!" Her mom crossed her arms.

"OK, I'm going!" Caroline said, leaving the study. "My bed is already made." She stomped up the stairs with Sammy behind her.

When she got to her room, she shut the door and lay down on her quilt. It was so unfair.

Her dad had maps, and strange objects made of stone and wood, and old books about giants and other creatures. But she was never allowed to look at them without his permission. And he never gave his permission, even though she was eleven.

"Double digits!" Caroline muttered, repeating Mom's words.

Well, they couldn't stop her from going down to the study later that night. She would

9

find out more about the Amber Giant whether she was allowed to or not.

She pulled out a notebook with a map of the world on the front. It was her log book. Her dad had one too, and showed her how to properly write down her observations like a real archeologist. It was mostly filled with boring facts about which birds she could hear in the morning, and if Dad said anything cool on the phone.

The last log read:

10:10 AM Saturday

We had pancakes for breakfast. Me: 3, Sammy: 3, Mom: 2, Dad: 5. Dad picked up the phone just after. He said 'mountain giant' and 'ancient legend'.

Caroline wrote a new entry:

4:30 PM Sunday

Sammy and I snuck into Dad's study. We found a book. The Amber Giant.

Caroline closed her eyes, and pictured the cover of the dusty book. The creature's forehead was heavily creased. It had a serious face — not mean, it just looked like it was thinking about something a little sad.

Could a giant be sad?

And why did her dad have a book about a giant?

She took out her red pen and circled today's entry. She wrote the initials RFI for 'requires further investigation'.

She would find out more about the giant, even if she had to hide in the study all night.

Chapter Two

After dinner, Caroline watched a film about the upper Himalayas with her family. Dad wanted to watch it, and Caroline only agreed because she thought there might be something about the giant in it.

But the film was boring. It was filled with scenes of grey rocks and snow. The people looked friendly though. They were often smiling with tan faces, and most wore colorful scarves.

The mountains were pretty, but nothing grew on them.

Caroline liked the Georgia mountains better. That's where they went on vacation. Those mountains had green plants and bright birds flying through the trees.

When it was time to sleep, she crept into bed without a fuss. Her mom and dad kissed her goodnight, but as soon as they were gone, she pulled out a flashlight to read. She was too excited to feel sleepy, and kept thinking about the book about the giant.

When everything was quiet and the clock read 1 a.m., she crept down the stairs, trying not to make a sound.

The Amber Giant book was right where she left it, sitting on top of Dad's desk.

The face on the cover was a little scary in the yellow glow of her flashlight. She realized for the

first time that the giant had fangs. A low, sad moan made the hairs on the back of her neck stand up. When she looked around, there was nothing that could've possibly made the noise.

Maybe it came from the book?

Caroline was afraid, but she remembered what her dad always said: "Fear often means there is something fascinating around the corner. Brave explorers will keep exploring, while lesser explorers run away."

Goose bumps covered her arms, but she was determined to go on. She carefully cracked open the book and flipped through the pages.

The book slipped out of her grasp and fell open to one page. A lot of the words on it were long and hard to pronounce. A picture of a giant figure against the wall of a mountain caught her eye.

Looking closer, she saw that the creature was trapped in the wall.

"Poor giant," she thought. Then, "Peak E-6, Annapurna." She said the words under the picture aloud.

Annapurna?

She thought back to the documentary about the Himalayas. She was sure it was a mountain range there.

"Like father, like daughter," came a low voice from the doorway.

Caroline jumped. Her heart beat rapidly, and she crouched behind the desk. A crazy thought flashed through her mind: *was it the giant?*

The floor squeaked, and something came closer. She shut her eyes tight.

"Caroline?" The warm, gentle voice was familiar. Opening one eye very slowly, she found her father.

"Sorry I scared you," her dad said. Then he rubbed the top of her head, messing up her already messy curls.

"Dad! I was just–" Caroline breathed unevenly, and tried to calm down. "For a second, I thought you were the giant."

"The giant, hmm?" Her dad peered at her. "So, the Amber Giant keeps you awake at night, too?"

Caroline touched the drawing of the creature and asked, "Is he in the Himalayas?"

Dad's fine, straight hair was neat as always, and flopped over his eyes when he studied the picture. She wished she had his hair rather than her curly mess.

"What makes you think that?" Dad asked.

Caroline showed him the text under the figure.

"Annapurna, Peak E-6." He smoothed her curls down with his hand. As Caroline studied the page, she heard a whisper. It almost sounded like *find me.*

"Did you hear that?" Caroline asked her dad. Chills ran up her spine.

"Hear what?" Her dad took a post-it from a pile in the corner and stuck it to the page.

"Oh, nothing, never mind." Caroline had a feeling that the book was talking only to her. "Who is he?" Caroline traced the image of the giant, who almost looked like part of the mountain.

"Well, no one knows," her dad explained. "At least, not anymore. This creature lived a very long time ago. He's trapped in rock, asleep for at least a thousand years."

"Poor giant."

Her dad whispered, "Can I tell you a secret?"

Caroline nodded.

"I want to wake him up," Dad said with a smile. "I'd like to ask him some questions."

Caroline's eyes were huge. "To wake him up, will you go to the Himalayas?"

"If that's where he is, that's where I'll go." Her father pointed to a pile of maps in the corner. "I have other books that show he's in the Himalayas, so I've been studying the mountain ranges. I'm nearly ready to start the expedition."

He rolled out a map and showed her how to read the curves.

"Contour lines show you how high the peaks are," he explained. "E-6 is so high I will need a guide. And I might have to bring an oxygen tank."

18

"Wow." Caroline's heart beat faster as she investigated the circles around the mountain. She imagined being so high up she would need an oxygen tank.

"Can I go with you?" Caroline asked.

"What about the documentary?" Dad asked. "I thought you said the Himalayas looked dry and cold after our movie tonight." He laughed and pulled a curl of her hair. "Boring, even."

"That was before I knew *he* was there. Do you think he's sad?" She looked at the drawing of the giant trapped in the mountain.

"He isn't awake, sweetheart," Dad said. "So no, I don't think he's sad. Anyway, you can come with me. But only if your mother says it's okay."

"That's not fair! She'll never let me!" Caroline crossed her arms.

"That's because you're still too young," Dad said. "When you're older, you can come with me

on my adventures. Right now, you need to get to bed."

It wasn't fair.

Caroline knew she was old enough to go. But Mom would never let her. Not in a million years.

Chapter Three

In her dreams, Caroline walked holding hands with the Amber Giant. It told her stories about ancient mountains and old forests.

But she would never get to meet the giant in real life. Mom would never allow it.

Caroline sighed and padded down the stairs in her pajamas to the breakfast table.

Her bowl of cereal was full, and she stared at the colorful flakes getting soggy. Sammy ate like it was a race, and was almost finished with his.

He stuck his tongue out at her and laughed. Caroline didn't laugh. Today she felt like a grump.

"Caroline? Are you a sleepy girl?" Her mom's dark eyes looked into hers.

"No. Yes." She looked down into her bowl. "Life's so unfair."

"So, I guess that means you don't want to go?" Mom said.

"Go where?" Caroline asked, looking around at the three excited faces at the table.

"The Himalayas!" Sammy cheered. "Didn't you hear?"

"With Dad?" Caroline couldn't believe her luck.

Dad raised an eyebrow and grinned.

"Your mom and I discussed it this morning," he said with a mouthful of marmalade toast. "I need to do some surveying in the Himalayas.

We'll make a summer vacation out of it in Nepal."

"We'll ride an elephant!" Sammy waved his spoon.

"Can we climb the peaks with Dad?" Caroline asked.

"We'll explore Kathmandu," Mom answered, then poured Sammy some more milk. "Any higher can be dangerous for kids."

"The altitude, right?" Caroline remembered that from the film.

"That's right, clever girl." Dad beamed at her.

"And the Amber—" Caroline caught herself just in time. Mom didn't believe in giants, and got mad when Dad started talking about things like that.

Dad put a finger to his mouth to silence Caroline, then he winked at her.

23

"I'll have work to do on the trip," Dad said. "It'll be boring for you, so I'll leave you three for a week or so." His back popped as he stretched his arms overhead.

"Can I go with you?" Caroline asked.

"No, honey," Mom said. "The journey is much too hard for children. We'll have lots of fun exploring lower down. It's a lot greener at the base of the mountains. More plants and animals, things to see."

Caroline felt her heart sink. They would be so close to the mountains, but she wouldn't get to see the giant.

Mom smoothed down Caroline's curls. "It's time for another haircut, young lady."

"Mom, you're always telling me to act my age," Caroline said. "Now you tell me I'm too young to go exploring. I'm old enough, and I want to go into the mountains with Dad."

24

Caroline pushed aside her soggy cereal.

Sammy shook his spoon at her. "You are too young!" he said in a fake deep voice, making a silly face.

She had to laugh.

Getting to Nepal was at least *something*, Caroline thought. She would think of a way to get to peak E-6.

One way or another, she would be there when her dad woke the Amber Giant.

7:00 AM Monday

We ate breakfast together. Sammy and me, cereal. Dad and Mom, coffee and toast. We planned our summer vacation in Nepal. My mission: to go with Dad on his quest to wake the Amber Giant.

Chapter Four

Kathmandu wasn't dry and dusty at all. It was covered with green grass, trees and flowers. The empty mountain landscape they saw in the film was much higher up, in the peaks.

Caroline still had jet lag, even though they arrived in Kathmandu four days ago. Their apartment was on a noisy street, making it difficult to sleep. And when she did sleep, she dreamed of the giant. Alive and trapped in the

mountain, he called to her and asked her to free him.

Now it was warm and sunny, and she wanted to take a nap. But the city was too noisy for naps.

"Look, a monkey!" Sammy shouted.

A golden-brown animal shrieked at them from the steps of an old temple. Busy tourists snapped pictures and blocked Caroline's view of the monkeys.

"There will be more monkeys to see at the Monkey Temple," Mom explained in an excited voice as she read her travel guide. "It's up a hill, so we can take rickshaws there." Her mom took her and Sammy's hands and led them to the street while Dad hailed the little wagons attached to bicycles.

They climbed into the seats of the rickshaws. Caroline and her mom shared one, and her dad got in a second one with Sammy. Her dad

planned to leave the next day, and Caroline still hadn't figured out a way to go with him. But despite that, she was enjoying herself. Her new summer dress was decorated with yellow and blue flowers and it made her feel cheerful.

Though the seat was uncomfortable, and the whole rickshaw jumped with every bump in the road, it was covered with bright, orange fabric that came over their heads and protected them from the sun. The driver cycled through the busy streets while Caroline looked out from the shade.

People dressed in a variety of colors carried all sorts of things from the markets: silk cloth, chickens, and bags of fruit. Women wore long dresses called *saris*. People chatted to each other loudly in the streets.

Caroline was glad she had her log book. Every night she wrote the new words she learned in it – words like 'rickshaw' and 'sari'.

"Your dad will leave early tomorrow," Mom said. "But don't worry, he'll be back before we know it. Meanwhile, we're going on an elephant safari! Won't that be fun?" She adjusted Caroline's bright blue sun hat as the rickshaw climbed a hill.

Caroline imagined that riding an elephant would be fun, but the thing she wanted to do most was go with her dad. She felt as if the mountains called to her.

Distant peaks rose above the city.

"Well, here we are!" Her mom jumped down and helped Caroline climb out. The rickshaw driver cycled around looking for more riders.

"There are loads of monkeys here!" Sammy cheered, and ran close to some seated on a

29

stone step. He had scrapes on his knees from jumping off low walls and landing on them, but he climbed up a stone platform anyway.

"Sammy, stay near to us!" Mom called.

Caroline looked around in wonder. Three enormous, golden statues sat on high pillars, and there was a tall building with painted eyes. Dozens of monkeys scurried around.

"Let's go see what they are selling," Mom said, and took Caroline by the hand.

Sammy and her dad stayed behind, taking pictures of the monkeys and the statues.

Caroline followed her mom to a tiny stand with lots of colorful scarves and bags.

"Would you like anything, Caroline?" Mom asked. "If you see anything you'd like, we can get it."

Caroline felt the soft, colorful bags, and let the smooth scarves cover her hand. Her eyes

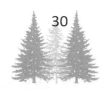

rested on a stone figure of a person with long arms, and legs like a dancer.

"This is nice." Caroline felt the stone. It was smooth and cool.

"How much?" Mom asked the woman behind the table. The vendor was an old lady with a brown, wrinkled face and a dark red sari. Her black hair was tied back tightly.

"That one is not for sale." The woman frowned.

"It's so beautiful," Caroline said. "So smooth." When she tried to give it back to the vendor, the stone doll's leg looped around her wrist. No matter what she tried, it wouldn't let go.

"It won't come off." Caroline showed her mom.

"How on earth did that happen? Well, let's see." Her mom tried to pull it off her hand, but it got tighter around her wrist.

After a few failed attempts to pull the doll off Caroline's arm, Mom asked the vendor how to get it off.

"You take it," the old woman said. "Take it and leave." The vendor waved her hands. "Free, free. Shop closed."

"What? Is there a trick to get it off her wrist? Don't you want to be paid for it?" Her mom waved some money at the woman, but the vendor covered her head with a yellow silk scarf and hid her face.

"No, it belongs to your daughter now." After making a strange hand signal, she leaned close to Caroline and whispered, "What is lifeless has life."

"What?" Mom leaned closer to the stand, but the Nepalese woman hurried away.

Caroline felt the stone leg loosen, and easily took it off her wrist.

"What a strange woman," her mom commented, and pulled Caroline towards the statues. She started to explain what the statues were, but Caroline wasn't listening.

The stone figure was warm to the touch.

Chapter
Five

Caroline couldn't sleep. The sounds of traffic, all the shouts from the street below, plus all Sammy's snoring kept her up.

At least her bed was comfortable.

She took the stone figure from her bedside table and stroked the smooth surface.

It was cold.

She wondered if it really happened. Had the stone really turned warm? Did its leg really loop around her wrist?

34

It was probably just her imagination. And jetlag.

Her dad was on the phone all evening, and she never got the chance to show it to him.

"What is lifeless has life," Caroline whispered. Sammy's snore had finally quieted down, but the doll was more interesting than sleep.

The stone grew warm in her hand.

"So I didn't imagine it." Caroline squinted in the dim light.

The figure had no eyes or face when she bought it. But now it opened two big eyes, and smiled with a mouth Caroline hadn't seen before. Surprised, she dropped it on the bed.

"Don't be afraid," it said in a voice as smooth as honey.

"No, I'm not afraid," she said, but she did feel afraid. She moved to the edge of her bed,

35

far from the doll, and hugged her knees to her chest.

"I'm just a magic piece of stone," the doll said. "I am the life of a giant."

"The Amber Giant?"

"You know us?" The mouth smiled and the eyes crinkled.

"My dad is going to wake him up." She crawled closer to the doll. It stayed where it was.

"The giant, if he awakens, will take back his life," the doll said. "I will return to mere stone once again."

"Oh. So you'll die?" Caroline whispered, hoping Sammy wouldn't wake up. Sammy would scream so loud if he saw a talking doll. But she didn't have to worry, because he was snoring loudly again, in a deep sleep.

"I don't know." The doll stretched again. "It feels good to move after so long."

"I want you to meet my dad," Caroline said. "He'll know what to do."

The doll shook its head.

"Only you can see me move," the doll told her. "Only you can hear me talk."

Caroline picked the doll up. It seemed warm and flexible, not hard like stone. She studied the little grey arms and legs.

"*Ar adat lichen adat*," the doll said softly.

"What does that mean?" Caroline repeated the words to herself, so she would remember them. With one hand, she pulled out her log book from the little bedside table and wrote them down.

"It's an old language," the doll explained. "It means *that which is lifeless has life*. Like me!" The doll stood up and wobbled in Caroline's hand.

"I said those words and they woke you up," Caroline whispered.

The doll lost its balance, fell back into Caroline's palm and closed its eyes. Its face looked peaceful.

"One more thing…" The doll opened one eye. "The giant should not be awakened. It sleeps for a reason."

"What reason?" The stone was growing cooler in Caroline's hand.

"That is all." The doll closed its eyes again. Its features disappeared, leaving smooth stone where there was a face.

The stone was now cold.

Wondering whether it was a dream, she lay wide awake until she heard her dad moving around the house just before the dawn.

38

Chapter Six

Caroline stood in the doorway and watched her dad prepare his bags in the tiny living room. It was before dawn, and the sky out the window was silver-blue. Dad wore a fleece, though it was a warm night. The bags were too full for the last scarf and book he tried to cram in.

"Gonna be cold. Might need the text, so it's got to fit, too," Dad said as he tried to zip the backpack closed.

"Dad?" Caroline's whisper made him jump.

"Did you come to say goodbye?" He pressed his knee on the pack to smash everything down, trying to make it all fit. The book wouldn't go, even though he tried several different ways.

"What does '*Ar adat lichen adat*' mean to you?" Caroline asked.

"Where did you hear that?" Dropping the bag, he came over to look her in the eye.

"I'm not sure you would believe me." Caroline shifted on her feet. Then she handed him the smooth doll, which was still and lifeless.

"Try me." He took the stone figure, his forehead wrinkled in confusion. "What's this?"

"A doll I bought at the market," Caroline explained. "Well, we never actually paid for it."

Dad gave her a strange look.

She told the story of how the figure wrapped its leg around her wrist. And how later, it spoke to her.

"A magic artifact!" He traced the doll with his finger, but it didn't move or wake up. "It spoke of the giant, you say? How wonderful!"

"So you believe me?" Caroline asked.

"Of course! These things are described in old books," Dad said with a gleam in his eye. "I have never seen one before."

"So – I can go with you?" she asked.

"You have to," Dad told her. "If this artifact has attached itself to you, it may be key in waking the giant. But your mother will never understand. Remember, she doesn't believe in giants or magic."

"But I have to come with you," Caroline pleaded. "You just said I have to go." She pulled her dad's pack. "I can help carry things."

"Well, I agree you should come. Am I right that this doll will only speak to you?"

Caroline nodded.

"Well, you won't be able to walk all the way. I'll have to ask the guide to carry you."

Forgetting to be quiet, she clapped her hands and sang: "We're going to the mountains! We're gonna wake the giant!"

"Shh!" Dad looked nervously towards the dark bedroom. "Don't wake your mom. We'll leave her a note. And you can't come in your pajamas. It will be cold in the mountains. Go put on your heaviest clothes. You can borrow a fleece from me. And a hat. Do you have gloves?"

"No." She wondered if the little doll would need warm clothes too.

"We'll buy them on the way." Her father turned back to his pack.

"Dad?"

"Yes, sweetheart?" He was already taking things out to make room for her clothes.

"The doll said not to wake the giant."

"Well, sweetie, we don't know much about the doll. And we shouldn't believe what it says. The Amber Giant can tell us a lot about life 1,000 years ago, including magical artifacts like the stone doll. That's why it's important to wake him."

Dad studied the figure. She wished the doll would speak, but it didn't wake up.

"Yeah, maybe the doll doesn't know what she's talking about."

"The doll told you a message from another time," Dad explained. "It's like voice mail. Only, we don't know who left it."

Her dad shook the doll, but Caroline took it from him.

43

"That doll isn't really alive," Dad said. "You know that, right?"

Caroline nodded, "I know…voice mail." But the doll had seemed so real. Maybe the doll was more than just voice mail? They'd probably find out more about the doll — maybe even from the giant himself, Caroline thought.

Excitement filled her. She couldn't believe she was going on a real adventure.

As Caroline searched through her drawers for a sweater, she frowned. The drawer was full of summer skirts and T-shirts.

Caroline slammed the drawer shut, then jumped nervously when it banged.

If Sammy woke up, he would want to come with her. Luckily, he kept snoring.

And hopefully her mom hadn't heard anything, either.

44

Dad rushed into her room and hurried her up. Light pink clouds appeared through the window, warning it was time to leave.

Alarmed at her summer wardrobe, Dad explained that they would have to buy winter clothes on the way. They had a long journey ahead, and it was better to leave as soon as it got light.

Chapter Seven

After walking for four days, they were deep in the mountains. It got colder as they climbed. Snow came to her ankles, and she stepped high to clear it. Her new boots pinched, but at least her legs weren't tired.

Caroline's new fleece, wool gloves and hat felt thin. She wished she had two pairs of gloves.

Their new guide, Pemba, had carried her much of the way. He was so strong. She was

46

amazed to see him race ahead of her father, even with her on his back.

But now he put her down to walk by herself.

"Little one, you must move or you'll get cold!" Pemba's grin was so big that she had to smile back.

Her hands were numb and her feet felt sore, but it didn't matter. She was on a real adventure.

The mountains were harsh and beautiful.

Some of the paths came close to a drop. One wrong step could send her falling to the bottom. She couldn't wait to tell Sammy about the narrow paths and sheer drops. Her log book was full of drawings of huge peaks and steep cliffs.

The snow covering the rocky landscape was so bright she needed to wear her sunglasses. They were so high, it seemed like they were

47

walking into the deep, blue sky. They passed lakes so clear that clouds reflected in them.

Around noon, they all stopped for some hot, buttery tea.

"Thanks, Simba." Caroline gratefully took a metal cup of the thick tea, dusted snow off a cold rock, and sat down.

"It's Pemba, not Simba," their guide told her. "Simba is a lion from a movie. I am a *Sherpa* – a guide." The Nepalese man laughed.

"Sorry, Pemba." Caroline's face grew hot, though the rest of her was ice cold. It was hard to remember his name. But she was too cold to take her gloves off and write it in her book.

Caroline shivered. "Are we almost there?"

"Getting higher. Girl getting colder," Pemba said, then looked at her dad.

"I have another fleece you could wear," Dad said as he felt her cheek. "It's big, but you'll be

48

warmer. We just have one more day before we get to the peak. I have to do some work tomorrow. After all, it's the climate survey that pays the bills." Her father held out an empty cup for a refill.

"Does that mean I can sleep late?" Caroline asked. The sleeping bag was warm in the morning, and she hated getting out of it so early. They usually started walking just after dawn.

"Yes, you can sleep in," Dad agreed. "Only, I promised you would call Mom." The buttery tea left a yellow mustache on her dad's stubbly lip.

Caroline made a face. Her mom was furious that she was on the expedition. All Mom did was worry about the snow and cold, so it was no fun to talk to her.

"When do we get to the giant?" Caroline asked. Sadly, the last drop of tea was gone. She

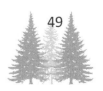

quickly pulled off a glove and cleaned out the yellow film in the tin cup with her finger.

Pemba shook his head.

"You should forget this monster," the guide said. He looked directly at her dad.

"Why?" Caroline asked. "He's the reason we came all the way up here. Why forget about the giant?"

Pemba didn't answer.

"We'll get there soon," Dad reassured her. He patted her arm, and handed her a large fleece. It fit like a dress. The sleeves went past her hands. The blue material came down to her knees, but she felt warmer right away.

"It's good, thanks." Caroline smiled at her dad.

"That's my girl," Dad said and beamed back. "An explorer just like her father." He threw a strong arm around her shoulders.

50

"If you don't want the girl to become an icicle, we better keep walking," Pemba said. "If I carry her, she will freeze for sure. She walks too." Then he strode off, and they had to hurry to catch up with him.

They walked for hours. Soon the sun was about to disappear behind a mountain peak.

Pemba found a good place to pitch the tents. Dad helped set up camp while Caroline rubbed her arms and shivered. Her legs were weak and tired. She just wanted to curl up in her sleeping bag for days.

Her dad made her eat two protein bars and drink two cups of tea. Finally, she was allowed to sleep. It took only a few seconds before she found herself dreaming of the giant.

"Release me," he moaned.

The giant's eyes stared at her, brown and kind. He looked so sad, and struggled against the rock.

Caroline clutched the doll to her heart as she slept.

When bright morning came, Caroline stretched her warm fingers and toes.

Finally, she had time to herself. And the energy to awaken the doll.

"What is lifeless has life," she whispered to the little figure.

The doll warmed up instantly. The heat felt good on her palm.

"*Brr*! It's cold in here," the doll said.

"We're in the mountains, near the giant," Caroline whispered. She didn't know if Pemba was near, and she didn't want him to hear.

"Ah, I can feel it. I feel stronger!" The doll stretched.

"Well, that's good, right?" Caroline pulled the warm sleeping bag around her and the doll.

"Not if you plan to wake the Amber Giant." The doll's blue eyes blinked. "Remember what I told you. It sleeps for a reason."

"Why should we let him sleep?" Caroline asked. "What's so bad about waking him up?" Sudden hunger cramped her stomach, and she devoured a protein bar. Three more were next to her sleeping bag.

"I do not know," the doll said. "I only know doom follows the waking of the giant." The doll's eyes grew enormous, and dominated its face.

"My dad says we shouldn't listen to you," Caroline said as she unwrapped a second protein bar. "He says you're like voice mail. A message from the past."

"I am *alive*," the doll told her. "I fear the giant, though I am part of him."

"Will you return to stone if he wakes?" Caroline whispered.

"I might not. I have had life so long, perhaps some of it is mine." The doll shivered. "I am too cold and must sleep again. If your father wakes the giant, will you promise me something?"

"Maybe. What is it?" She swallowed the last bite of the bar.

"Say the following words, *para en ras*," the doll said. "Now you try."

"*Para en ras*."

"Perfect!" The eyes and mouth of the doll grew round with surprise.

"What does it mean?" Caroline asked.

"Just say it." The doll yawned and stretched its little arms above its head. "I'm getting sleepy. Perhaps we will not meet again."

"Wait! Don't go!" Caroline said, but it was too late. The doll's eyes disappeared just as a

cold rush of air startled her. Dad's red face pushed into the tent. Short, light brown hair showed on his cheeks and chin.

"Just a couple more hours of surveying and we can go," Dad told her. "You ate two energy bars – good. Eat one more, then call your mom."

"Do I have to?" She frowned.

"She's already angry. Don't get me in any more trouble, OK?" He grinned and pulled his face out of the tent, zipping it back up.

Her hair was greasy, so she positioned the wool hat so none of her wet-looking curls would show. The Miranda/Mom button was the favorite Skype contact on her dad's smartphone. She pressed it, and her mom's worried face instantly appeared.

"Caroline? Are you OK?" Her dark eyes searched through the screen.

"Yes, I'm fine. See? Breakfast." She held up a protein bar.

"That's all you're eating?" She sounded near panic.

"They're good enough, Mom," Caroline said. "I had two already. And there is Pemba's butter tea." She spoke through bites.

"Pemba the guide?" Her mom's eyes got closer to the screen.

"That's him." Caroline nodded.

"Where is he now?" Mom's voice was getting higher. Not a good sign.

"I don't know. Dad's out surveying, so maybe he's helping."

"You're alone out there?" Her mom ran her hands through her hair, messing her curls up further.

"Mom, it's not like there is anyone around to bother us," Caroline pointed out. "We're in the

middle of nowhere." She moved the phone around so Mom could see the cozy, orange tent around her. "Outside our tent it's just rocks and snow."

It wasn't the right thing to say. Her mom's face paled.

"What was your father thinking?" Mom said. "Of all the crazy ideas…"

"Mom, I'm fine! It's fun here."

Sammy ran into the view, wearing a T-shirt with 'Safari' printed on it.

"We're having more fun than you!" Sammy said. "We rode an elephant!" His freckled face filled the screen.

"What was it like?" Caroline couldn't help smiling. He looked so happy.

"Smelly! Why are you wearing a hat?"

Now she could only see one big, blue eye.

"Because it's cold," she told him. "Back up, I can't see your face."

"In the tent? It's cold in the tent?" Mom pulled Sammy onto her lap. Her worried frown contrasted with Sammy's excited grin.

"Not really," Caroline said. "It's just better with the hat on, that's all."

"It looks dumb," Sammy shouted. "You shouldn't wear a hat inside."

"Well, I like it," Caroline told him. Her new hat was almost too colorful, with blue, pink, red and yellow stripes. Her new gloves had the same cheerful pattern.

"When are you coming back home?" Mom's eyes got closer to the camera, and showed up big on the screen. "Caroline? If you want to come now, you just say the word. I'll send the police."

Caroline nearly laughed out loud.

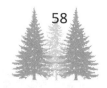

"We just need to do something here, then we'll turn around," Caroline said. "Dad says it will only take three days to get home. Going down is faster."

"Three more days! With no real food?" Mom's worried face filled the phone screen. "What that man was thinking, I just don't know…"

"Mom, I have to go," Caroline said. "The milk tea is ready." Caroline had no idea if the tea was ready, but it seemed like a good way to get off the phone.

"Do you have any signs of altitude sickness?" Mom asked.

"What? No!"

"Nosebleed? Dizziness?"

"Bye, Mom. Bye, Sammy." Caroline waved, and watched Sammy spinning around while

59

shouting, "I'm dizzy! I'm dizzy!" before she hung up.

With a deep sigh, she decided to face the cold for some of the Sherpa's rich, buttery tea. Before she even climbed out of her sleeping bag, her father unzipped the tent. His face was flushed and his eyes shone.

"I found him! I found the Amber Giant!"

Chapter Eight

He was bigger than she expected, and darker. The giant towered over them, as tall as a house. His hands were the size and shape of large, hairy rocks. She couldn't see the giant's face. It was too high, and was pointed at the mountain peaks in front of him. Its fur wasn't golden, but a muddy brown.

Caroline leaned in close, wrinkling her nose at the smell.

61

"He's breathing," she whispered.

Groaning and creaking came from its hairy chest.

"Why do you say that?" her dad whispered back.

"Listen!" Caroline could clearly hear its lungs working. But her dad shook his head.

"I can't hear anything," Dad said.

Their guide was back at the tents. He refused to get near the creature.

"Why is he so brown?" Caroline asked. "In the book, he's gold."

Long, matted fur covered the giant's body.

"He's probably just dirty," Dad said. "Covered with 1,000 years of dust."

"Are you going to wake him?" Caroline's voice shook with excitement.

"That's what we're here for." Dad rubbed his hands together, his breath quick.

Caroline took the doll out from a pocket in her fleece and held it to her chest.

"I hope you don't die," she whispered to the doll.

"*Ar adat lichen adat*!" Her dad's voice echoed.

Nothing happened.

"Guess it didn't work," Dad said. "Maybe my pronunciation is off?" He opened his mouth to try again, but there was no need.

The mountain rumbled.

One of the giant's fists uncurled, and pieces of rock and stone crumbled away from it. A larger rock tumbled out from the wall when the giant bent his knee.

Caroline clutched the doll tightly.

"It's crumbling!" Dad shouted. "We have to get clear of the rocks!"

The giant gave a mighty roar that shook the mountain wall.

Caroline yelled, *"Para en ras!"* Then she ran down the path with her father, who was soon gasping for air. When they stopped a good way from the falling rocks, he took deep breaths.

"I can't believe it! The Amber Giant is awake!" Dad hugged her, he was so excited. "This is a wonderful moment!"

Caroline looked down at the doll. It had a face, and seemed to be asleep.

"Can you see this?" She showed her dad the doll.

"Your doll? Of course." Her dad scanned the path they had just run down, but the giant hadn't followed.

"No, its face! Don't you see?" Caroline grinned, the cold air stinging her gums. "She didn't die!"

64

"I don't see a face," Dad said.

She was about to wake the doll up when strong footsteps shook the rocks around them. A huge figure appeared on the path.

Caroline felt its heavy steps as it moved towards them. Her heart beat quick as a clock gone crazy.

"Dad! Maybe we should run?" Caroline pulled at her dad's hand, but he only stared at the giant.

"No. I want to talk to him," Dad said.

Caroline slipped behind her dad.

The giant's hands were big enough to crush them both. Its feet crunched rocks and turned them into dust.

"*Parate juru!*" her dad shouted to the giant. "Welcome, friend."

Caroline wrinkled her nose.

The giant smelled of old leather and wet dog, and it looked like it could step on them and crush them. Caroline held her father's hand.

The giant kneeled down.

It bent its head to look at her dad.

Despite the cold, Caroline started to sweat when it peered around her dad to see *her*. Caroline's heart pounded harder when the giant met her eye.

"Brave explorers will keep exploring," she whispered to herself.

The giant's brow was big and bumpy. It had a lot of hair on its cheeks and chin, and its eyes were dark brown – just like in her dream.

Only, they weren't kind eyes.

They were hard and a little mean.

"Caroline!" The giant's voice was so loud she wanted to cover her ears.

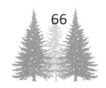

Caroline blinked. She tried to speak, but no words came out.

"At your service," the giant roared. Then he bowed.

"You speak English?" Her dad was astonished. "How can this be?"

"Ask her." The giant pointed to Caroline.

Too surprised to talk, Caroline could only wonder in amazement. This enormous creature, apparently, was at her service.

What on earth was she going to do with her very own giant?

Chapter Nine

"That which is lifeless has life," Caroline said for the third time, but the doll did not open its eyes. Her dad and the giant stood next to her in the snow and watched. Dad was quite tall, but he barely came up to the giant's hairy knees.

"Pemba." She rubbed her arms for warmth.

"What?" Her father was in his most serious and grumpy mood. He had tried to ask the giant questions about life 1,000 years ago, but the creature didn't remember anything.

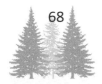

68

"Maybe our guide will know what to do." Caroline's teeth chattered.

"I just can't understand why the giant speaks modern-day English." Dad was lost in his own thoughts, and stared at the creature's face, high above his own.

"I speak English!" the giant shouted, then he pointed a hairy finger at Caroline. "She speaks English!"

Dad rolled his eyes. "Clearly. Tell me, how many people lived in these mountains before you slept?"

"People lived here. Yes. Mountains like this." The giant grinned, showing his fangs, and looked around the peaks fondly.

Her dad slapped his head with his hand. "All that study, for nothing. We will learn nothing about the past through this creature. I should never have come to wake him."

69

The giant's eyes narrowed. "Not wake me?"

"It's not his fault that he doesn't remember," Caroline said. Without thinking, she petted the Amber Giant's huge, furry hand. Clouds of dust rose into the air, and she wiped her glove on a rock.

"Ick." Caroline held her nose. "You should take a bath."

"Bath! Your wish is my command." The Amber Giant jumped to his feet, causing a small landslide.

"Hey! Where are you going?" Caroline yelled up to the giant, as she held on to her dad's arm.

"To find a lake!" The giant stomped off.

Both Caroline and her father lost their balance and fell on the cold, icy rocks.

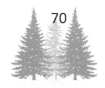

"Ouch!" Caroline rubbed her left arm and leg. Even with long underwear and thick wool pants, the fall hurt.

"He'll do anything you say?" Her father's mouth hung open.

"I guess so." Caroline shrugged. "Though I don't know why."

"It must have something to do with the doll," Dad said. "I think you're right, Caroline. We should find out what Pemba knows."

They walked quickly back to the tents. The only lake her dad knew of was 100 miles away, so who knew when the giant would return.

When they reached their little camp, Pemba scowled at them.

"Giant walks, rockslides start," Pemba said. "Bad news, a giant in these mountains. We are not safe. It was foolish to wake it." Their guide crossed his arms and frowned at her dad.

71

"But the creature does as my daughter asks," her dad said. Then he unzipped the orange tent and pulled out binoculars to scan the mountains.

"What? How can this be?" Pemba peered at Caroline, his brow furrowed.

"We hoped *you* would know, Pemba," her dad said. "Caroline, show him the doll."

She passed him the stone doll.

The guide took his glove off and held the figure.

"Yes, it is warm. This is an important doll." Pemba held it close to his eyes.

"I heard you call out words when the giant woke up," her dad said. Then he scanned the rocky landscape. There was still no sign of the hairy giant.

"*Para en ras,*" Caroline said. "The doll told me to say it." Caroline clapped her gloves

together. She hated standing around, it made her so cold.

"It means, *you are bound to me*," Pemba explained. He handed her the thermos of buttery tea.

Caroline gratefully poured herself a cup of the thick, hot liquid. It tasted sweeter every time she drank it.

"Clever girl!" Pemba grinned. "We can kill the giant! First, we must destroy the doll. Then he will be weak."

"No!" Caroline and her dad shouted at the same time.

"The doll is my friend." Caroline tried to take the stone figure back. "And the giant hasn't done anything wrong!"

"We can't just destroy a relic from 1,000 years ago," her dad said. "There is much we can

learn!" Her father also tried to grab it, unsuccessfully.

Pemba shook his head and tucked the doll into his own pocket.

"That giant killed whole villages long ago," Pemba told them. "What was life like 1,000 years ago you ask? Just like it is now. Mountains stood here, families lived and died. People ate, fought, and laughed. But 1,000 years ago, a giant lived here with an evil master. He killed hundreds of people. Luckily, a witch made him sleep. Until now."

Caroline and her dad exchanged a look.

"Why didn't you tell me this before?" Her dad rubbed his forehead. "We could have at least brought a tranquilizer."

"I told you to forget about the giant," Pemba said. "You should have listened."

Caroline hated hearing grown-ups fight. She

finished the tea with a loud slurp.

"We will go back to Kathmandu now," Pemba said. "We will gather the other Sherpas. Then we will hunt the giant."

"But he's a good giant!" Caroline shouted. "He won't hurt anyone!"

"No, little one. This giant is bad," Pemba told her. He started to dismantle the tents, a big frown on his face.

"Dad, what if the giant comes back?" Caroline scanned the snow and rock landscape in the distance. "We have to warn him!"

"We're running out of food," Dad said. "And you've been shivering for the last two hours. It's too cold for you up here. We have no choice but to go with Pemba."

The mountains were empty.

There was no sign of the Amber Giant, and there was no way to warn him.

Chapter Ten

Caroline's mother ran to her and hugged her so tightly she couldn't breathe.

"You're so skinny!" Her hands grabbed at Caroline's elbows and shoulders. "I can feel your bones through the fleece."

"Did you bring me anything?" Sammy jumped up and down. "Why is your hair all matted?"

"It's not like there are showers in the mountains, silly." Caroline took a grey rock out of her pocket. "I got this rock for you. It's from the highest peaks."

"Wow! From the tippy top of the Himalayas!" Sammy ran in circles, holding the stone. "Is it true you drank yak milk?"

"Yak milk?" Caroline peeled off her fleece, finally feeling warm in the summer sun and lower altitude. Her arm was bruised from her fall on the ice, so she tried to keep it hidden.

"Pemba's tea," Dad said. He had uneven stubble that made his face look dirty. "We weren't sure we should tell you, so your mother and I decided to keep it a secret. It's made with yak butter." He tried to give his wife a hug, but she stepped away.

"David, you and Caroline stink," Mom said. "But before we go home so you can shower, we need to talk. Kids? Sit on that bench in the shade there while your dad and I discuss something.

Oh, and Caroline, eat this." Her mom handed her a sandwich.

Caroline sank gratefully on the bench, choosing a sunny spot. Her legs were tired from all the walking. Somehow downhill was even harder, because she had to concentrate so she wouldn't slip. She was glad Pemba carried her much of the way, even though she was mad at him for taking her doll.

She took one bite of the sandwich, and it tasted so good that she ate it all in a few seconds. Then she wanted either another sandwich or a nice, long shower.

She was thinking about which one she wanted more when she caught Sammy staring at her.

"Why did you eat so fast?" he asked.

"I'm really hungry," she explained. "I only ate power bars. And that…yak tea."

Sammy swung his legs as he examined the stone. He didn't take his eyes off it and seemed completely enchanted with it.

Caroline grinned. She knew the look on Sammy's face. She suspected he was imagining amazing adventures. She decided to give him an exciting story, so he would know the stone was very special. But she wouldn't tell him about the giant. Not when she didn't know if he was going to be killed by Pemba, or if he was safe in the mountains. Sammy would get too upset if he knew the Amber Giant lived, but then died so soon after.

Caroline decided to tell him part of the story. "It was actually a very dangerous adventure," Caroline said. "But don't tell Mom, OK? She'd really freak out if she knew how easy it would be to fall to our instant death with just one wrong step off the path."

"I won't tell," Sammy said. "Pinky promise."

Leaning in close, Caroline said, "And the tents could have blown off the mountain if they weren't held down by stones like that one. I think that stone there saved my life."

Sammy's eyes grew wide.

A few steps away, Mom gestured energetically as she spoke with Dad in the shade of a tree. Caroline hoped she wasn't too angry. At least her mom smiled when she returned to the bench.

"Now that we're all together again," Mom said, "we'll have dinner at one of the best restaurants in Kathmandu. I've been hoping to try it before we leave." Her mom pulled Caroline up and gave her another bone-squashing hug.

Sammy ran ahead yelling, "Instant death!"

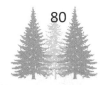

"Sammy, please!" Mom shook her head, her forehead pinched.

Caroline and her dad took long showers at the apartment. After, the whole family walked over to the restaurant.

Colorful paper flags hung from the ceiling. They ordered lots of little dishes to share with rice, and momo, the traditional dumpling of Nepal.

Sammy chatted about how bumpy and smelly the elephant ride had been. Her mom and dad held hands, though her mom frowned a lot. She kept giving Caroline more food, so that she couldn't even keep track of how many dumplings she ate.

Caroline pushed a momo around on her plate. She wondered what the poor giant was doing now.

"Are you all right, Caroline?" Her mom felt her cheek. "You haven't said a word all through dinner."

"Just tired," Caroline said, which was true, but not the real reason for being quiet. She was sad about the giant and her doll, and worried what would happen to them.

As soon as they got home, Caroline crawled into the little bed next to Sammy's. He was already snoring when her dad came to tuck her in.

"OK, my little explorer, what's wrong?" Dad patted her arm, and she winced when he touched a bruise.

"What's going to happen to the doll?" Caroline asked. "And the Amber Giant?" A tear slid down her cheek.

"Oh that – hang on a minute," Dad told her. "I have something that will cheer you up."

He left the room and came back with her stone doll.

"My doll!" Caroline sat up, feeling more awake.

"When Pemba was sleeping on the trail, I stole it back," her dad whispered.

Caroline hugged the doll. Now that the doll was safe, her bruises didn't hurt anymore.

"This means they can't weaken the giant by destroying the doll," Caroline said. "But they can still hunt him, right?"

"I have already sent messages to my fellow academics," Dad told her. "We are seeing what we can do to save him. The Amber Giant is a historical rarity, a gem from another time. I am sure we can find some law that protects him. So everything will be OK. Right?"

Caroline nodded, feeling a little more positive about the situation. Dad smoothed her hair and kissed her forehead.

The bed was soft and snug around her. She was warmer than she ever felt on the trail, and soon fell asleep.

Chapter Eleven

Caroline woke up in the middle of the night so hungry she had a stomach cramp. Sammy was snoring softly in the bed next to hers.

Padding out to the kitchen, she heated up a few momo from dinner. She ate five before a huge face at the window made her drop her fork.

"Giant!" Caroline said, much too loud. She hoped Mom wouldn't wake up, since she would never understand.

Caroline ran to the window and lifted it open.

The giant's golden-brown fur shone in the moonlight. His eyes were hard, like glass. They weren't like the kind, soft eyes she imagined in her dreams at all.

"I took a bath," the giant roared. "At your service."

"*Shh*! Speak quietly," Caroline whispered. "Everyone's sleeping."

"Not everyone is sleeping," the giant said, then wrinkled his leathery forehead. "Not fireflies, not bats, not you, and not this giant."

Caroline touched his soft, clean beard, which was long enough to come through the window.

"You look much better," Caroline told the giant. "You're such a nice color."

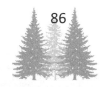

86

The giant blinked, his hard eyes softening a little.

Though their apartment was on the second story, the giant stood firmly on the sidewalk. He didn't even have to tiptoe for his face to reach the window.

"Listen, there are some people who want to kill you," Caroline explained, trying to keep her voice down. "You should hide."

"Let them come. I will kill them first," the Amber Giant said. "Humans are my enemies." He made a big, hairy fist. "Except you."

"No! No killing." Caroline leaned on the windowsill and looked into his leathery face, framed by a mane of golden hair.

"No killing?" The Amber Giant looked confused. "But my old master said we must kill. He said that was my purpose." Hairs growing from his great nostrils shook as he spoke.

"Well, I am your new master," Caroline explained. "And I say do not kill anyone. All right?" She shook a finger at him.

"Of course. My new master says no more killing. So I will not kill." The giant blinked his dark eyes.

"And you better hide before the Sherpas find you."

"Hide? Where?" The giant's long, golden beard came into the window, and he moved his big head through it.

"No, you can't come in!" Caroline said. "My mom would freak out! And the apartment is way too small for you." She pushed the giant's rough face back out the window.

"Then you come out." The giant's voice was loud, as if it echoed off mountains. "You and I will run now." The giant put a large, hairy hand

over Caroline's small wrist. His grip was tight and started to hurt.

"Ouch!" Caroline pulled away, but it made her wrist hurt more. She winced at a sharp pain.

"OK, giant." Caroline calmed her voice so she didn't wake anyone. "I'm your master and I say, *let go of my wrist*!"

The giant loosened his hand. Caroline rubbed her red wrist and part of her arm.

"That really hurt, you know."

"I hurt master?" The giant's eyes grew wide.

"Forget it," Caroline told the giant. "Listen, you have to go by yourself." She pointed out the window, past the rooftops of the city. "Go back to the mountains!"

"Caroline?" Her father came to the window. "What's all the noise?"

He gasped when he saw the giant's huge face just outside.

"Oh, he's beautiful!" Dad said. "No wonder they called him the Amber Giant."

"This is my dad," Caroline explained. She tried to rotate her hand, but it was too painful. "He woke you. Remember?"

"What happened to your arm?" Her dad took her arm gently, but let go when Caroline winced.

The giant peered at him.

"Yes, I know you," the giant said. "You ask many questions."

"Sorry about that." Dad leaned closer to the giant. "I just want to know about life here a long time ago. Was it this cold in the mountains? Do you remember more or less snow?"

"There is always snow here," the giant agreed. "More or less."

Her father sighed deeply.

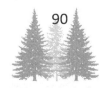

"I was just telling the Amber Giant he should hide far away," Caroline told her dad. "The Sherpas are looking for him."

"Yes. You should hide," Dad said. "But where can he go?" His face suddenly lit up. "Wait! I have an idea!" Her dad disappeared into the living room. Caroline heard the sound of papers being moved around.

The giant opened his mouth to speak, but she shushed him as soon as Mom's voice called out.

"Honey, are you coming back to bed?" Mom called from the bedroom.

"Just helping Caroline get something to eat!" her dad called back from the living room.

"Oh good, she's eating," Mom said, sounding happy. "Feeling better, Caroline? Want me to come help?"

"No, I'm fine, Mom!" Caroline called. "Dad's got it. I'll go back to sleep in a minute!"

Caroline turned back to the giant.

"My mom can *not* see you," Caroline whispered to the giant. "We can't let her. She would never understand you're a good giant."

"Am I?" the Amber Giant asked. "But I hurt master." His dark eyes stared at her little wrist. It was turning a dark blue.

"You didn't mean to hurt me." Caroline stroked the giant's beard with her good hand. "You're just very strong."

Her dad raced into the kitchen holding a map.

"See this peak?" he asked the giant. "You can hide there. It's very hard for even a Sherpa to get to."

"I cannot understand the drawing." The giant shook his massive head.

A scream rang out.

Caroline looked out the window to see a woman shouting in Nepali, and pointing at the giant. Two teenage boys ran out of an alley and fell on top of each other in surprise.

"You have to go!" Caroline pointed to the map. "Dad, is that the highest peak?"

"No, it's not the highest," Dad said. "Oh, how do I explain it? Giant, do you understand north and west? What about miles, do you know what those are?"

"Stars," the giant answered. "I understand stars."

Then he roared. The teenage boys and several men were throwing things at the Amber Giant.

"Stones! They throw stones!" the giant shouted. "I eat attackers!"

Lights came on in several of the buildings along the street. More screams and yells pierced the night.

"No, don't hurt them," Caroline pleaded. "You have to run away."

"What's all that noise?" Mom called out.

"You have to go to peak E-6, where we found you," Dad told him. "Then follow the north star." Her dad quickly drew a sky map with a few constellations in it.

"I know that sky." The giant nodded. "Ouch!" He roared again.

"Is that the furnace?" her mom called from the bedroom. "Is the heater making that noise?"

"No, Mom, go back to sleep!" Caroline yelled.

"Follow this for a while, until you get to a very tall mountain peak," Dad explained. "Then follow this star. That should lead you far away

from where people can go." Then he handed the paper to the giant.

The giant stuffed the star map in his mouth, chewed, and swallowed. After a mighty burp that smelled like sour plants, he looked expectantly at Caroline.

"We go now. Stones hurt." The giant's dark eyes shone.

"No, I can't go with you," Caroline said. "I'm too small. I wouldn't survive in the mountains."

"You want me to go—" His eyes grew big. "Alone?"

Caroline touched the giant's cheek. "You must go alone. Or they'll kill you!"

"My master doesn't want me," the giant sobbed. "I hurt master! My master!"

The Amber Giant ran down the street, scattering the people. The street cracked under the giant's weight, but he didn't step on anyone.

95

Tears slid down Caroline's cheeks as she watched the Amber Giant disappear into the night. Dad held her tight.

"You did the right thing, Caroline." Dad kissed the top of her head and examined her wrist when she showed it to him. She couldn't move it much at all.

"What is going on?" Mom appeared in a flowery robe, rubbing her eyes.

Out the window, people were screaming and crying. Some ran down the street in the direction the giant went.

"Just a local fight," Dad said. "Nothing serious. It upset Caroline, though."

"Poor girl! She's just so tired from that trip," Mom said. "I told you she was too little to go with you." She took one look out the window, then closed the curtains.

"No, it was OK. It was fun," Caroline said. "It's just hard to come back to a noisy city." Her voice choked up as she remembered the beautiful mountains, the white snow and bright blue sky. Hopefully, the giant would be happy there, in a place he belonged.

"See? She's like me." Her dad stroked her hair. "We belong out there, exploring the world."

"Well, right now this one belongs in bed," Mom said. "Caroline! What happened to your wrist?"

"I, um, banged it on the window," Caroline said. She hated lying, but there was no way to explain a giant at the window. Her wrist was turning a deep purple.

"That must have been some bang. It looks like it could be sprained. We should go to the

hospital." Her mom's voice was high and strained.

"How about we try my magic arnica gel to see if the bruising goes down?" Dad used his most soothing voice. "If it's still bad in the morning, we'll go to the hospital."

"That sounds good," Caroline said. "I'm too tired to go to the hospital now." All she wanted to do was curl up in bed and cry. She felt terrible that the giant left thinking that she hated him.

Caroline allowed her mom to lead her back to her bed, and tuck her in. She waited for her dad to come in with the gel. Her wrist burned.

A long, sad moan from far away sounded in the night.

"The giant must be so lonely," Caroline thought. Quietly, she sobbed to herself. Thankfully, Sammy was still asleep in the other bed.

98

She feared she would never see the Amber Giant again. She hoped he would be safe in the mountains.

There was no way she could help him now.

Their last two days in Kathmandu, she couldn't do much because of her sprained wrist. And because she was so tired. Her mom spent a whole morning with her at the hospital while they x-rayed her arm and wrapped it in a splint.

News of the giant's nighttime visit made the local papers, but most thought it was a big dog, or possibly a yak that had frightened people so much. The Sherpas stated they would hunt the giant, but the newspapers did not take them seriously.

Caroline was worried about the giant, but she was also afraid it would come back to find her.

It was a relief when they got on the airplane to return home. At least she could stop worrying the giant would show up at her window. Though she felt awful that she didn't get the chance to tell him that she cared about him.

At least she had the doll.

Bringing it out of the country was the best thing she could do for the giant. She would keep it safe, and the giant would be okay.

Once she got home, Caroline thought about the giant every day. Her dad gave her the book, *The Amber Giant*, that she had discovered in his study. And she kept it by her bed. Each night she hoped the giant was safe, and that he wasn't too lonely.

Three years passed before she returned to Kathmandu.

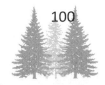

Chapter
Twelve

The city was just as noisy and busy as she remembered. Caroline and her dad dropped their bags at the hostel, then navigated to Freak Street by foot.

"Why is it called Freak Street?" Caroline yelled over the sound of a rickshaw rattling past.

"No one knows. But it's a good name!" Her dad led her down a narrow street that opened into a square. It looked just like the postcard in her hand. She hoped to find the author in that very place.

The postcard read:

Dear Caroline,

I am a Sherpa, and a friend of your large, hairy acquaintance. He needs your help. If you come to Kathmandu, ask for Michael Sherpa near Freak Street. I hope to see you soon. Bring the doll.

Yours,

Mike and Hairy

A stall caught her eye. It was decorated with a banner of a large, hairy giant in the mountains. She grabbed her dad's sleeve and they made their way to the vendor's stand.

The little dolls sold at the stall had amber fur, though otherwise looked like men. T-shirts with HAIRY HERO OF NEPAL came in two colors: yellow with orange writing, and red with black print. A cartoon of a smiling face with long hair was printed on the T-shirts.

"Who – or what – is this?" her dad asked the young Nepalese man behind the stand.

"Have you heard of Sasquatch? Yeti? The Abominable Snowman?" the vendor asked, talking fast and with a big grin. "There are many legends of large creatures who walk the mountains around us. Of course, they don't really exist."

"Well, I'm not so sure they don't exist," her dad argued. The Sherpa stopped talking at once and quietly looked away.

"We're looking for Michael Sherpa." Caroline waved the postcard. "Or is it Sherpa Michael?"

"Caroline?" The young man came around to the front, where they stood.

"Yes, that's right." She was surprised he knew her name.

He bowed to her. "Good to meet you. I am glad you have come. We don't tell the real story to tourists, and try to keep this between Sherpas only. But know that your giant friend is a hero to us. He saved a party of twenty explorers, including three Sherpas. They would have all died in an avalanche. But our friend dug them out and returned them to safety." He smiled, his teeth bright against his smooth, tan skin.

"Really?" Caroline smiled. "See, Dad? I knew he was a good giant!"

"But also know this, Caroline. The Amber Giant is very ill. Too long has he been separated from the doll that contains part of his life." The Nepalese man shook his head, looking serious.

"I have the doll. It's safe," Caroline told him, and patted her colorful purse.

The vendor clasped her shoulders.

"You save many people if you save him." He let go of her shoulders and bowed again.

Caroline blushed.

Dad put a protective hand on her shoulder.

"So you are Michael?" Her dad raised an eyebrow. "The one who sent Caroline the postcard?"

"No, I'm not Michael." The vendor shook his head. "He's a friend of mine. I will tell him you are here when I see him this evening. Where are you staying?"

Her dad handed him the card with the address of their hostel.

Caroline examined the "Hairy Hero" doll. The golden fur looked so soft. She remembered the giant's broken-hearted expression, his eyes full of tears, when she last saw him running away from the town.

"Is the giant in danger?" Caroline asked the vendor. "I mean, the last time we were here people wanted to kill him."

"Kill him? Oh no!" the vendor said. "He's a friend to us all. I will tell Michael – Mike - to find you. One more thing…"

The young Nepalese man looked intensely at her. "The giant thinks you hate him. He is very sad about this."

Caroline opened her mouth to say something, to explain that she loved the Amber Giant, but the man waved his hands.

"No, no, don't explain," he said. "Just be nice to him. Tell him he's a hero, and that you care about him. Can you do that?"

Caroline nodded.

"Good." The man smiled and held up a HAIRY HERO shirt. "Now, since you're here, how about buying a little something to take back home?"

"Sammy would love the orange and yellow one," Dad said. He found a kids' medium. "What do you think?" Caroline nodded. It was perfect for Sammy.

"I'll take this doll," Caroline said. "It looks a little like him." She picked the soft toy up, and was relieved when it didn't move or grow warm. It was just a normal doll. The toy had a smile on its face. She hoped the real Amber Giant would forgive her.

Chapter
Thirteen

They spent the rest of the afternoon searching for a scarf for Caroline's mother. After a tasty meal of momo dumplings, it was time for a good night's sleep.

A Nepalese man greeted them as soon as they reached the front lobby of their hostel. He looked ready for the mountains. Caroline wondered if he was hot in his wool hat and gloves.

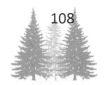

"I'm Mike," he said with a bow. "A good friend of our big hero."

"Are you the one who sent the postcard?" Caroline set down her colorful bag. It dug into her shoulder, and she was tired from carrying it around all day.

"Yes. It is good that you came." His face was solemn.

"Is he OK?" Caroline asked.

"He is getting weaker," Mike said. "Too long has he been separated from part of himself."

"The part in the doll?" Caroline drew the stone figure out of her bag.

Mike's eyes lit up. When he moved to touch it, Caroline's dad blocked the move, taking the doll for himself.

"I'm sorry," Dad explained. "When we left here three years ago, there was talk among the Sherpas about killing the Amber Giant. We

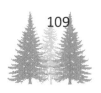

know the doll would be useful in destroying our big friend, as you call him." Her dad's blue eyes were bright and intense.

"Dad! Mike's his friend!" Caroline's eyes flashed.

"No, no. Your dad is right to suspect," Mike said. "At first, it is true that we could only see evil in having a–" The Nepalese man looked around to make sure no one was listening. "–*giant* in the mountains. But he has a big heart. Our friend has saved many Sherpas and adventurers."

"See?" Caroline urged her dad to show Mike the figure, but her dad shook his head.

"All the same," Dad said, "I'll keep this on me for now." He slipped the stone doll into his backpack.

Mike shrugged. "It's OK. I don't need to carry it. We leave tomorrow at dawn. Be ready for the mountains. And Caroline?"

Sherpa Mike's serious face made her nervous.

"See if you can mend his broken heart." He bowed and left the hostel, leaving Caroline with a sad pain in her chest.

Did the giant really think she hated him?

"Well? If we're leaving that early," Dad said, "we'd better get some sleep." Dad studied his sturdy National Geographic watch. "We have to be ready in just about six hours."

Anticipation quickened Caroline's heart. They would be in the mountains tomorrow. And soon, they would see the Amber Giant.

The next morning, Caroline found herself walking through snow from dawn until the sun was high above the peaks. Her thighs were tired from the climb, but it was not as difficult as she remembered. Stepping easily, she didn't feel

111

the snow pulling at her feet like before. She remarked on it to her dad.

"Well, you're bigger now, Caroline." Her dad grinned.

"Sherpa Mike takes you on a gentle path," Mike said, slowing down his pace to match theirs. "It is narrow and icy, so go slow. The Hairy Giant will meet us soon."

"This low down?" Her dad scanned the tallest peaks, which towered above them. "I thought he'd be safer up there."

"I told you, he's safe from us," said Sherpa Mike. "He's a friend to Sherpas."

"It's just that our guide Pemba was so angry we woke the giant," Dad explained. "He was set on killing the Amber Giant, and destroying the stone doll."

"Pemba is one of the people our giant saved from an avalanche last year. Sherpa Pemba has

changed his mind, and even donates money to help us buy medical supplies for the Amber Giant," Mike explained.

"Medical supplies?" Caroline asked with concern.

"The giant has had some skin problems and recently needed antibiotics, too." Mike's eyes grew wide. "He needed a lot of expensive antibiotics. He's a big giant!"

"Is he OK now?" Caroline asked.

"He is a little weak," Mike warned.

The path grew even narrower. Caroline walked close to the mountain wall, away from the drop-off. She would have to tell Sammy how dangerous it was to walk here. He would love hearing about it. She could make it sound really scary, though she wasn't scared.

The Sherpa pointed to a clump of rocks.

A flash of gold shone at the top of the rocks.

A huge figure moved out of the shadows, revealing himself.

Caroline's heart stopped. She had forgotten how enormous he was. His amber fur was thin, unlike the thick mane she remembered.

"He looks sick," Caroline said. "But he's still beautiful." She caught her breath as the sun shone red highlights in the giant's fur.

As the giant walked towards them, tiny pebbles scattered and the ground vibrated. But he walked gently, and no one had to hold onto the rocks to remain standing.

When he knelt down and bent his great head, his eyes looked kind. They were warm and brown, just like in her dreams.

Caroline's heart melted.

"Master has returned after so long." The giant's voice was low.

"Yes, I'm sorry I couldn't come before," Caroline said. "I didn't know you were sick." She pet the giant's arm, and fine hair came off.

"Your hair is falling out!" She gasped at all the fur on her glove.

"You left me," the giant said. Great tears filled his eyes.

"I'm sorry. I didn't want to," Caroline told him. "I was too young to stay. My family was returning home, so I had to go with them. But I thought about you every day."

The giant's great lip quivered.

"They brought something for you." The Sherpa nodded to her dad, who revealed the doll.

Her dad lay the doll near the giant's feet.

The Amber Giant gasped. "My doll!"

"The girl kept it safe for you." The Sherpa patted the giant's massive hand. "If she had

115

stayed here, the doll would have been destroyed."

"That's right. I kept it safe," Caroline told him. "I took it far away from here, to another country because I love you very much." She took one of the giant's hands in both of hers.

The giant's moist eyes stared down at her.

"I have heard all the stories of what a wonderful hero you are," Caroline said. "You're the best giant ever."

"Do you really think so?" His voice was faint.

Caroline nodded.

"But I remember…" The giant pointed at her left wrist, and he took a deep, shuddering breath. "I hurt Master!" Great tears ran down into his beard and froze there.

"I'm not hurt at all." Caroline waved her hand around. "I didn't even bruise." The second part

wasn't true, but she wanted the giant to feel better.

"I'm a bad giant," the Amber Giant said. He kicked the doll to the edge of the path, then crept back behind the rock. The doll was dangerously close to the cliff edge.

Caroline moved quickly to rescue the doll. Her hiking boot landed on a patch of ice, and she slipped and fell on her back. Before she knew it, her legs were dangling over the cliff.

"Caroline! Don't move!" Dad's voice was loud with panic.

There was nothing to hang onto, and she started to slide. *Now* she was scared.

Her dad and Sherpa Mike tried to grab her, but both were too late to rescue her.

She managed to turn around so her belly faced the cliff wall, and held on. She hung from

two rocks wedged into the cliff wall, unable to climb back up to the path.

"Giant!" shouted Sherpa Mike. "Please come out. We need your help!"

Caroline dug her fingers into the rock, holding on as best she could. The whole mountain wall shook when the giant came towards her.

"Master?" The gravelly voice reached her, but she was afraid to look up.

"Please, help!" Her voice shook. "Help me." Her fingers were getting tired. She couldn't find anywhere solid to put her feet.

"I don't know how?" The giant looked confused, even scared. "I will only hurt you again."

Loud shuffles indicated the giant was walking away. Caroline's fingers dug into the rock. Her arms burned. She would not be able

118

to hang on much longer. She had to do something, or she would fall to her death.

"You won't hurt me!" Caroline called to the giant. "I promise, you won't hurt me."

The footsteps stopped.

"I'm your master, and I say, help me up!" Her voice came out stronger this time. She took a shaking breath in, and felt two strong hands grab her forearms.

Next, she was in the air. Then she was lightly placed on her feet.

Her dad wrapped his arms around her and hugged her so tightly she couldn't catch her breath. When he let go, Sherpa Mike hugged her too, squeezing very tightly.

Gasping, she looked up at the giant.

His eyes were open and round. He studied his hands.

119

"I saved you? I didn't hurt Master?" The giant knelt down and peered at Caroline.

"You saved my life!" She threw her small arms around one of his massive arms. He was much too big to hug around the middle.

"I'm not—" The Amber Giant looked happy. "I'm not a bad giant?"

"No, you're a great giant." Caroline kissed his hairy arm, getting golden fur in her mouth.

"Now will you take the doll?" Sherpa Mike picked up the stone figure and held it up to the giant. "If you get better, you can save many people."

"If Master wants me to, I will." The giant stood up and stretched. "I can be a stronger hero."

"Please, take the doll," Caroline said. "Become well again." Her legs felt weak, so she

sat down very close to the mountain wall, far from the path edge.

"Take this, girl." Sherpa Mike gave her a cup of warm yak butter tea from his thermos.

Her dad sat next to her, and she leaned on him as she drank.

"OK, I will be well again. I will eat the doll!" The giant grinned, showing two fangs. He shook icicles off his beard.

"Wait!" Caroline wiped the butter mustache off her lip. "What do you mean *eat*?"

"No, I have colleagues here in Kathmandu who wanted to see it!" Her dad's cry was ignored by Sherpa Mike, who handed the doll over.

"To health!" The Amber Giant raised the stone figure to his mouth.

Caroline covered her eyes with her hands.

121

A crunch echoed through the mountains. When Caroline dared to look, the head of the doll was gone. Great teeth broke the stone with loud, cracking noises.

The giant's eyes brightened.

"I feel stronger!" He blew stone dust as he continued to eat the rock figure.

"So strong." The Sherpa's eyes were wide.

Dad's mouth hung open as he watched the giant finish off the doll.

The Amber Giant burped so loudly that Caroline had to cover her cold ears. A huge cloud of old, sour plant smell filled the air.

"Ugh." Caroline sneezed. "Is she – is the doll dead now?"

"She's just a message, Caroline," Dad said. "Remember? Voice mail." Her father pinched her arm.

"No, not dead," the Amber Giant said. "Part of me. In me."

Stone crumbs caught in his beard.

"I can hear the doll inside me. She says she was wrong." The giant picked a pebble from his teeth and crunched it.

"Wrong about what?" Caroline breathed more deeply as the cool mountain air replaced the smelly burp.

"About waking me," the giant said. "She says it was a good thing your father broke my sleep."

"See, Dad? She's not just an answering machine," Caroline said. "Voice mail doesn't apologize."

"Many of us think the same," Sherpa Mike said. He stroked the giant's arm, his blue glove picking up golden fur. "It was a good thing to wake you."

"You're a hero!" Caroline stood up, stronger after the yak tea.

The giant reached out his hairy arms and hugged her very gently. He smelled like old, musty paper in the forgotten corner of an attic.

"I am a gentle giant." He smiled with his great, yellow teeth. "I save humans. That is my purpose. But will you leave now? Then I will be sad again."

"I've been thinking..." Her dad collected stone crumbs from the giant's fur. "I'm on a project at work that will take me to the Himalayas once a year, every summer. We're doing a climate study, along with some mapping of the region. Caroline can come with me and help out with the measurements."

"Here? In the mountains?" Caroline looked around at the bright, unspoiled blue sky that contrasted with the snowy peaks around her.

124

"Every summer?" The giant's eyes filled up again.

"That's wonderful!" Caroline clapped her hands together.

The giant breathed in deeply.

"Every summer I will see Master!" the giant said. "I feel so happy, I want to run now!"

"OK, but remember–" Sherpa Mike shook his finger. "Run *down low* so you don't start an avalanche."

"Now, promise me something before you go," Caroline said as she cleaned off the amber hairs that clung to her glove.

"Anything for Master!" the Amber Giant said.

"I know you will always be a good giant, Caroline said. "But can you also take a bath from time to time?"

"Next time you see me, I will be clean." The giant grinned, showing his fangs. Then he ran off, happy once more.

The ground shook, and a small landslide had everyone holding onto each other. Caroline, her dad, and Sherpa Mike ended up in a heap on the ground.

"The Amber Giant has not run for many months." Sherpa Mika laughed. "He must be feeling better."

"He doesn't know his own strength," her dad said, dusting himself off.

"I have a lot of work to do with him," said Sherpa Mike. "But don't worry, he'll continue to be the Amber Hero. We are talking about a statue in the main square."

They made their way back to the city.

Caroline was sad to leave the beautiful mountains so soon, but she knew she would be

back in a few short months. Sherpa Mike said she was a true mountain girl — especially after surviving that fall.

When they got to Freak Street, she bought a scarf for the giant. There weren't any hats or gloves in his size.

"The Amber Giant doesn't get cold." Mike fingered the wool scarf, which was a nice blue color.

"Yes, but if a lost hiker sees him coming," Caroline said, "our friend would look a lot less scary wearing a scarf." She thought the color would go well with the giant's fur.

"I like your thinking, girl!" Sherpa Mike's eyes brightened.

"Yes, she's a smart cookie," her dad said, and gave her a hug. "And brave."

"Will the Amber Giant be OK?" Caroline gazed above the buildings around her, but she couldn't see the mountain peaks.

"With friends like us, he won't just be OK," said Sherpa Mike. "He'll be protected and cared for." He offered his house when they next visited, so they wouldn't have to stay in the hostel. He promised to send Caroline postcards updating her on the giant's activities.

And she made a vow to visit every summer.

9:14 PM, Wednesday

Kathmandu, Nepal

The Amber Giant is well. And I will get to see him every summer! Sammy turns eleven in a month. Double digits! He's old enough to know the story of The Amber Giant. I am going to write it all down for him as a birthday present.

About the
Author

Giulietta M. Spudich enjoys writing everything from children's stories to grown-up fiction, and poems in between. She lives in Cambridge, England where she moved from California in 2002. She is inspired by cats, especially her late black cat, Smokey.

Find Giulietta on Twitter @spudichpen.

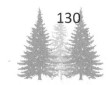

Thank you for reading *The Amber Giant*.

Handersen Publishing is an independent publishing house that specializes in creating quality young adult, middle grade, and picture books.

We hope you enjoyed this book and will consider leaving a review on Goodreads or Amazon. A small review can make a big difference for the little guys.

Thank you.

More books from
Handersen Publishing, LLC

The Evil Mouse Chronicles (Middle Grade)

Middle Grade

Picture Books

Also from Handersen Publishing

Cover Art By
Raven Howell

Interview with
Author, Alex Henson

Featured Authors
Alex Henson
Rebecca Linam
Scott Merrow
Theodora Morley
Jeffrey G. Roberts
Elizabeth J.M. Walker
Sephone Zorro

Featured Artists
Rhea Baxter
Allen Forrest
Jane Gregoritch
Jessica Hillegeist
Raven Howell
Denny E. Marshall
Cesar Valtierra
Matthew Wall
Shannon Wall

Featured Poets
Jana Bataineh
Raven Howell
Ginny Kaczmarek
Herb Kauderer
Denny E. Marshall
Peter MacQuarrie
Phillippa Rae
Lily Tierney
Damian Wakefield

Stinkwaves
Magazine
Spring 2017
Volume 5 Issue 1

Short stories, poetry, and illustrations from
contributors of all ages from around the globe!
www.stinkwavesmagazine.com